WITHDRAWN

Tucky Jo
and
Little Heart

To Kentucky Johnnie Wallen and his family
and all of the brave soldiers who honor their country

SIMON & SCHUSTER BOOKS FOR YOUNG READERS
An imprint of Simon & Schuster Children's Publishing Division
1230 Avenue of the Americas, New York, New York 10020
Copyright © 2015 by Patricia Polacco
SIMON & SCHUSTER BOOKS FOR YOUNG READERS is a trademark of Simon & Schuster, Inc.
For information about special discounts for bulk purchases, please contact Simon & Schuster Special Sales
at 1-866-506-1949 or business@simonandschuster.com.
The Simon & Schuster Speakers Bureau can bring authors to your live event. For more information or to book an event,
contact the Simon & Schuster Speakers Bureau at 1-866-248-3049 or visit our website at www.simonspeakers.com.
Book design by Laurent Linn
The text for this book is set in Minister Std.
The illustrations for this book are rendered in two and six B pencils and acetone markers.
Manufactured in China
0816 SCP
2 4 6 8 10 9 7 5 3
Library of Congress Cataloging-in-Publication Data
Polacco, Patricia, author, illustrator.
Tucky Jo and Little Heart / Patricia Polacco. — 1st edition.
pages cm
"A Paula Wiseman Book."
Summary: A fifteen-year-old soldier in World War II meets a sweet young girl in the Philippines
who helps him remember what he is fighting for as he helps her and others of her village avoid starvation,
and many years later she returns his kindness.
ISBN 978-1-4814-1584-2 (hardcover) — ISBN 978-1-4814-1587-3 (ebook)
[1. Soldiers—Fiction. 2. Kindness—Fiction. 3. World War, 1939–1945—Philippines—Fiction.
4. Philippines—History—Japanese occupation, 1942–1945—Fiction.] I. Title.
PZ7.P75186Tuc 2015
[Fic]—dc23
2014004223

Tucky Jo

and

Little Heart

PATRICIA POLACCO

A Paula Wiseman Book

SIMON & SCHUSTER BOOKS FOR YOUNG READERS

New York London Toronto Sydney New Delhi

AUTHOR'S NOTE

A few years ago I was on the road doing school visits and staying at a hotel in Virginia. One evening as I walked down the hall to my room, I passed a banquet room with a military banner over the entrance. Inside, a reunion of World War II veterans was being celebrated. I leaned into the room and was struck by the sight of very old soldiers standing in groups exchanging stories of their tours of service in the Pacific. I stepped inside and soon was invited to join them. I was deeply moved both by their stories of bravery and heroism and by their love for one another. I was also impressed by their compassion for the people whose villages they had liberated during the war.

As I returned to my room that evening, I started thinking about some of the veterans in my own village and how compelling their stories must be.

The following account is a story that Johnnie Wallen related to me shortly before his death at the age of eighty-five in January 2010.

I will try to tell it as nearly as I can in his own words.

I was born in Allen, Kentucky, on October third, nineteen hundred and twenty four. I grew up like any backcountry boy in Kentucky. Tougher than last year's jerky and faster than a scared jackrabbit. I could whittle and carve just about any kind of stick or wood and I could sneak up on just about anything. Came right handy for huntin'. My pa taught me how to use a shotgun when I was knee-high to a grasshopper.

By my twelfth birthday I was known in three counties for sharp shootin'. I could hit the eye out of a gnat from a furlong away whilst I was on a dead run dodgin' a wild boar hog. I always took first prize over at the county fair for fancy shootin'. I even caught the eye of the sweetest little ol' gal, Freda Hall, from over Prestonsburg way. I knew when I was old enough I was going to spark her!

When I was ten or so, we heard all about the war that broke out in Europe and that feller Hitler. Then the papers said Pearl Harbor was bombed and we were at war with Japan in the Pacific. I told my Ma that I was fixin' to enlist in the army and go fight for my country. The onliest thing was, I wasn't old enough to join up. Even though I had promised my heart to Freda . . . I had to go. So soon enough my folks lied me older when I went to sign up. Sure 'nuff the army took me that very day. After my basic training I was assigned to the Sixth Infantry, Company G, Twentieth Division. Then we were deployed to the Pacific theater on the biggest ship I ever saw!

I was miserable sick the whole way. The onliest boat I ever seen was a river raft back home on Hominy Creek. Bein' the youngest recruit on that there ship, almost everyone aboard was callin' me "that kid from Kentucky," or just "the kid." At first I didn't like them a-sayin' that, but after I got to show 'em how good I was with a rifle and our sergeant picked me for special training as a marksman and for heavy ordnance—explosives—they all looked up to me. I later became part of a very special unit that went into the jungle to seek and destroy machine gun nests and enemy outposts. Then the "Kentucky Kid" moniker became a badge of honor.

I could hardly wait to land and get into the thick of the fightin'.

Almost as soon as we landed we were thrown into the worst of the conflict. I had never seen so much killin' and sufferin'. Our division was sent to so many places to fight that everything started blurring together. My outfit was known as "the Sightseeing Sixth" because we held the record for the most consecutive days of continuous combat! We fought tooth and nail . . . cheek to jowl! We were in Milne Bay, then Maffin Bay, then Lone Tree Hill, New Guinea; Muñoz; and finally we were on our way to Luzon in the Philippines. We had been battling for 219 days straight!

By the time we got to Luzon I was blind tired. So tuckered I could hardly put one foot in front of the other. I was plumb weary of the jungle. It was hot, steamy, stinkin', and thick . . . and the bugs . . . I never seen so many bugs! There was snakes, lizards, and big spiders too. It rained every day. The ground was always damp and mushy. Our feet never got dry. To think that I wanted in on all this fightin'. . . . Now I knew there ain't no glory in war. But I was in the army and it was up to me to take a stand and fight for my country.

But at night I'd have dreams about my ma and her bakin' powder biscuits. I could even smell the pine boards in our house . . . I could see the green grass in our holler. Oh how I wanted to be back home with my ma and my kin.

My unit's mission on Luzon was to clear the jungle to build an airstrip and also to level the land to bivouac and pitch our tents for an outpost. So just about every day I was swingin' a machete at thick underbrush and slashin' vines. One day I stopped for a swig of water from my canteen. The bugs were swarmin' all around me. Some of 'em were as big as my hand. All of 'em were stingin' me. I was being eaten alive. I was a scratchin' fool.

I had welts all over every inch of my skin. Some of 'em burned and hurt like bites from fire ants back home. Then I heard rushin' water. I pulled back the underbrush and saw a small native village just yonder from me at the bend in a river. I saw village women standin' knee-deep in the river tryin' to catch fish with their bare hands.

Then, sudden-like, I could feel someone behind me. I turned real fast and drew up my rifle. Standin' there like something out of a dream was a scrawny little ol' girl. She wasn't any bigger than a minute and looked weak as a fawn deer. I dropped to my knees and drank her in. Somehow lookin' at that innocent tiny girl gave me a peace that I hadn't felt in a long time. She reached out and touched one of the swolled bug bites on my arm. Then she bent down and plucked a plump leaf from a ground-huggin' plant. She broke it in half and squeezed the goo that was oozing out of it on the bite. It was instant, blessed relief! So's both of us picked them leaves and put the medicine that came from them on all of my bites.

"Thank you . . . thank you, little angel!" I whispered.

She just blinked at me. Didn't smile . . . didn't say nothin' . . . just looked at me with those beautiful haunted eyes.

"My name's Kentucky Jon," I said as I pointed to myself.

She cocked her head to one side.

"Kentucky Johnnie," I said louder.

She just stared.

"I got something you'll like," I said as I pulled a chocolate block from my K rations. I held it out to her. I knew she wanted it real bad, but she held back till I put it in her tiny hand. Then she stuffed the whole block into her mouth. I thought she'd choke on it! She chewed hungrily at it, barely taking breaths to swallow.

Then both of us just sat there for the longest time. It made me feel calm and less homesick to be there with her.

"Wonder what your name is," I muttered.

Then I noticed a small birthmark on her arm. It was shaped just like a perfect small heart. "Little Heart!" I sang out. "That's what I'm a-callin' you!" I whispered to her.

"Tucky Jo!" she suddenly blurted out as she pointed at me.

"Tucky Jo . . . Tucky Jo . . . Tucky Jo," she sang as she turned and ran back into the jungle.

I gathered up as many of them leaves as I could to take back to camp with me.

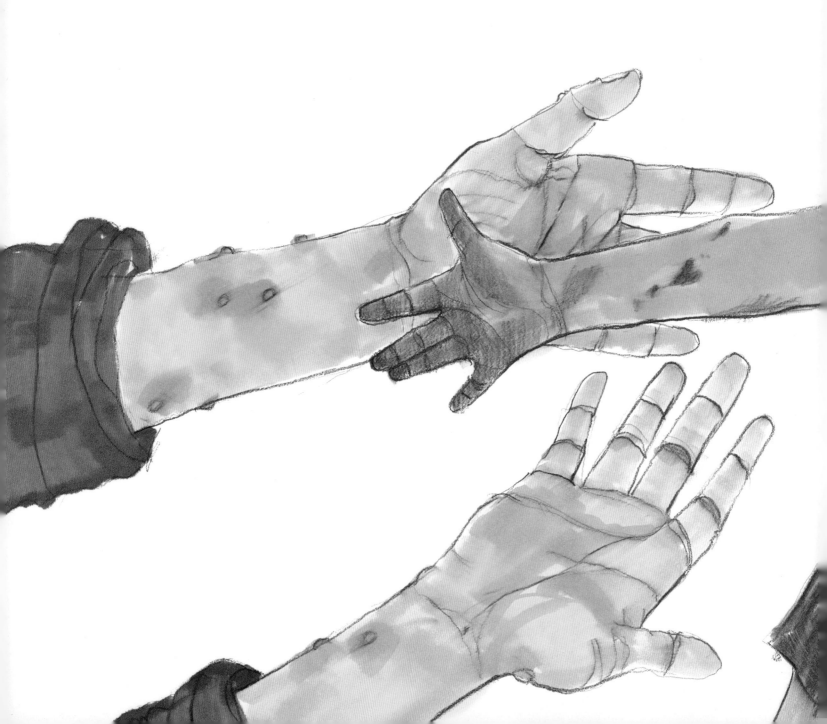

When I got back I showed the medics them leaves and how they made the bites better. Pretty soon them leaves were bein' used for to heal any kind of skin scrape. I figured it wasn't a good idea to tell anyone about Little Heart, bein' that sometimes natives were scouts and spies for the enemy. I guess I was afeared that our captain might think that . . . so I kept Little Heart as my own secret.

I spent most of that night whittling a hinged dancin' doll for that little girl. I'd made lots of 'em back home for my kin. We called these "jiggy dolls." Each arm and leg were wired at the elbow and knee so that when you shook it the arms and legs waved . . . like they were dancin'. Then I put the body and head on a stick. . . . I couldn't wait to see Little Heart to show her how to make it dance.

The very next day I made it my business to be in that same place where I first saw her. I waited and waited . . . and, sure 'nuff, she finally came. I pulled the jiggy dancer from my pack, attached the stick, and thumped it with my fingers. Sure 'nuff that little doll started dancin'. Little Heart couldn't take her eyes off'n it. Then she smiled. A smile so sweet and full of life that both of us clean forgot that a war was raging all over this island.

After that, almost every single day, I'd meet up with Little Heart so I could share my K rations with her. After a time I'd take along extra food so's she could take some back to her people.

She never tried to talk to me. I 'spect that she didn't know English. I'd seen a lot of kids over here that were shell-shocked by all the fightin' around them and they just plain stopped talkin', laughin', or playin'. Alls I knew was that I needed to see that little thing as often as I could. Somehow lookin' at her made all of the combat make some sort of sense. I felt like I was doin' all this warrin' for her . . . for kids just like her.

One day when I showed up at our spot, Little Heart wasn't there. I got real scared and sick inside at the thought that she might have come to harm. So I toted my pack full of my usual load of K rations and set out for her village. When I stumbled into her village with the food, no one was there. Then Little Heart ran out of a fallen-down hut and hugged my legs. Next, women, old men, and children poured out of their huts. Little Heart pulled me into hers.

There, settin' in a hammock, was a very old man that looked weary and spent.

"So you must be Tucky Jo. I'm Linus Zaballa," he said as he smiled.

"You can speak English!" I said, surprised-like.

"Of course I can . . . I learned it in school." He smiled.

Turns out that he was the onliest one that could.

"You have been very kind to my granddaughter," he added as he motioned to Little Heart.

I smiled at her. "She's an angel, all right. . . . Doesn't say much, though," I said.

"She hasn't spoken since she saw her mother killed by soldiers. Her father and brother were taken . . ." His voice trailed off. "Your name is the only thing she says."

"Do you folks see a lot of soldiers around here?" I ask, tryin' to gauge where enemy troops might be.

"No," he answered. "We were grateful to see them leave. We don't know where they are. . . . They took all of our young men and food. Now we are starving," the old man said as he cried.

"But you got a river right here. There must be a lot of fish in it," I said.

"They took all of our nets and fishing baskets. We have no way of getting the fish out of the river," he answered.

I thought for a minute.

"Have your womenfolk line the shore tonight . . . right at dusk. I promise you there will be fish, more fish than you can eat!" I called out as I ran for camp.

That evening I waited till the sun started settin'. I sneaked to the ordnance shed and got me an armload of dynamite and fuses and a charge box. I made my way to the river's edge just north of the village. I assembled a bundle of dynamite and set a long line of fuse and swam it out to a group of rocks in the center of the river. Swam back to the shore and connected the fuse lines to the charger. I waited till I could see the womenfolk line the shore. I set the magneto and pushed the plunger down.

BOOM . . . BOOM-A-BOOM! The water commenced to boil, then shot straight up into the air.

Fish started fallin' outa the sky. They landed all over the bank. Women and children were running back and forth gatherin' 'em up and puttin' them into their baskets.

They were laughin' and singin' as they did it.

From that day on they all called me "that boy who made it rain fish"!

They feasted on them fish for days. What they couldn't eat right away, they dried and preserved.

I even shot a water buffalo and butchered it for 'em so's they had fresh meat.

The whole focus of my life came to providin' for them people . . . that is, when I wasn't out on recons and fightin' the war.

After a time I told my sergeant about the village folks. He reckoned since they hated the enemy as much as we did they weren't spies, so he let the children come up to the fence line and even gave them supplies that were bein' airlifted in to us on the landin' strip we built.

Little Heart was my constant shadow. Almost everywhere I went, except for combat missions, she was right behind me.

Whenever I went to her village it felt like I was home . . . surrounded by my kinfolk.

Everybody in my outfit had grown to love 'em too.

Then one day my unit was rousted from a sound sleep earlier than usual. "Enemy troops are headed this way!" the sergeant barked. "High command has ordered firebombing of the jungle all around us . . . so we have to evacuate!" he added.

"Get up. Get up. We're bombin' the jungle!" he barked as he ran from tent to tent.

"Sarge, what about Little Heart . . . the villagers!" I called out in pure panic.

"Ain't got time, kid. Ain't got time to save 'em!" the sarge whispered.

"Sarge, if'n I run as fast as I can and gather 'em up and bring 'em here . . . can we evacuate them with our troops?" I begged him.

The sarge nodded his permission and I took off runnin'. I ran so hard and fast that I could taste blood in the back of my throat.

I arrived just in time and they all followed me back to the base. Some of the boys in my outfit picked them up and threw them into the back of transport trucks.

Little Heart was in my arms and huggin' me as hard as she could.

The bombs were screamin' into the jungle right behind us. Everywhere we looked there was fire.

"Tucky Jo . . . Tucky Jo," she cried as she hugged me even tighter.

I had to peel her off'n me and throw her into a transport truck. She screamed and screamed. I 'spect she only felt really safe with me . . . now I was takin' that away from her.

I started sobbin' and she reached for me and tried to jump out of the truck.

"No . . . Little Heart . . . you gotta go . . . you gotta," I sputtered.

Then the truck rolled out with a jerk. Her grampa held her back as she screamed my name. . . .

That's the last time I ever saw that little girl.

Finally the war ended and I went home to Kentucky. I had been wounded several times, but came home in one piece.

I ended up marryin' up with my darlin' Freda. We moved to Marshall, Michigan, bought a farm, and raised a family together.

She gave me eight beautiful children. We've been married for nigh on to sixty-five years now. I have twenty-four grandchildren, twenty-eight great-grandchildren, and even one great-great-grandchild.

But in all of these years I don't think a day has passed that my mind didn't fall on thoughts of Little Heart and set to wonderin' about her.

Now, like a lot of old soldiers, I been gettin' sick a lot these days. Spendin' much of my time at the veteran's hospital clinic over to Battle Creek way. Freda tried to get me in to see the specialists that could help me, but there was such a waitin' list we never seemed to be able to see 'em. I just seemed to be gettin' worse and worse. What was real hard to take was that my eyesight and hearin' was all but gone! Couldn't afford one of them newfangled hearin' aids and eye surgery was expensive. . . . Couldn't pay for it!

Then one day on one of my routine visits to the Veterans Administration a new nurse came into the room. She was soft and gentle and seemed to really care. She had my thick file in her hand. She opened it and studied it closely. "Is this a photo of you when you were enlisted?" she asked as she showed me an old wrinkled picture. "You were very handsome!" she said as she smiled.

"That's my Johnnie," Freda whispered as she stroked my head.

"I have some new medicine for you today, Mr. Wallen. . . . This will be a lot better than what you are using now," she said as she examined me.

"I've had a meeting with the specialists, and they have agreed to take your case. You need very specific medicines for your heart condition. They have prescribed the finest for you to take . . . ," she said as she listened to my heart.

"How much is all of this going to cost?" Freda asked.

"It is all being taken care of," the nurse said as she held Freda's hands.

"And how did you ever get Johnnie in to see the specialists? We've been on a waiting list for what seems like years. . . . We finally gave up hope," Freda cried.

"Why you doin' this for me, girly?" I asked as I searched the nurse's face.

"Because I'm taking care of you now . . . just like you did so many years ago for me. . . ." Then she leaned in to my face. "Tucky Jo will have only the best! *Only the best for you . . . my Tucky Jo!*" the nurse whispered as tears rolled down her cheeks.

She rolled up her sleeve and showed a birthmark on her arm. It was shaped like a perfect heart.

EPILOGUE

Nurse Zaballa was true to her word and saw to it personally that Johnnie Wallen received the finest care possible for the rest of his days. She later told him that she had been looking for him all these years and had lived in the hope that she could thank him for his kindness. It was because of him that she came to America. She attended nursing school, married, and became the mother of three sons. Two of them are practicing physicians and one is an engineer. She felt that none of this would have been possible had she not been saved and fed and cared for by her Tucky Jo. Her greatest gift to him was to order him the best and newest hearing aids. She also saw to it that he had cataract surgery. So for the first time in ten years he could see and hear!

Johnnie Wallen was one of the most decorated soldiers in his company. He received the following awards:

2 Purple Hearts

3 Bronze Stars

1 Bronze Arrowhead

The Asiatic-Pacific Campaign Medal

The Philippine Liberation Medal

The Korean Service Medal

The Combat Badge

A Good Conduct Medal

The World War II Victory Medal

But to Johnnie Wallen the medal that meant the most was a small silver heart on a chain that Nurse Zaballa gave him shortly before his death. He was buried with it pinned to his chest. On the back it was inscribed: *For my Tucky Jo from your Little Heart.* He passed in January 2010 at the age of eighty-five.